P9-DDU-891

"When I tried to give this back to you," I said, holding up my Spitzer medal, "you wouldn't let me. You told me that a Spitzer never quits. So we're not quitting."

"What do you suggest we do, Walter?" said the Major.

"Fight," I said, and the calmness with which I said it surprised me. "We're not giving up this house without a fight."

"Will surely delight readers."

—*Bulletin of the Center for Children's Books*

"Written in action-packed dialogue and illustrated with cartoonlike drawings, *General Butterfingers* [is] a good choice for hard-to-please elementary grade readers."

—*School Library Journal*

To Nate,

John R. Gardiner

General
Butterfingers

John Reynolds Gardiner

Illustrated by Cat Bowman Smith

Puffin Books

PUFFIN BOOKS

Published by the Penguin Group

Penguin Books USA Inc., 375 Hudson Street, New York, New York 10014, U.S.A.

Penguin Books Ltd, 27 Wrights Lane, London W8 5TZ, England

Penguin Books Australia Ltd, Ringwood, Victoria, Australia

Penguin Books Canada Ltd, 10 Alcorn Avenue, Toronto, Ontario, Canada M4V 3B2

Penguin Books (N.Z.) Ltd, 182–190 Wairau Road, Auckland 10, New Zealand

Penguin Books Ltd, Registered Offices: Harmondsworth, Middlesex, England

First published in the United States of America by Houghton Mifflin Company, 1986
Reprinted by arrangement with Houghton Mifflin Company
Published in Puffin Books, 1993

5 7 9 10 8 6 4

LIBRARY OF CONGRESS CATALOGING-IN-PUBLICATION DATA
Gardiner, John Reynolds.
General Butterfingers / John Reynolds Gardiner; illustrated by Cat Bowman Smith.   p.   cm.
Summary: When three aging war heroes are forced out of their home
by the wicked nephew of the now-deceased owner and former occupant
of the home, eleven-year-old Walter determines not to let it happen.
ISBN 0-14-036355-6
[1. Old age—Fiction.]   I. Smith, Cat Bowman, ill.   II. Title.
[PZ7.G174Ge 1993]   [Fic]—dc20   92-44487   CIP   AC

Printed in the United States of America
Set in Garamond No. 3

In Memory of Christial Branson — J. R. G.

To Eve, Alex, Ben, and Sue — C. B. S.

Acknowledgments

I would like to pay credit to Andrew J. Galambos for the many ideas and concepts of his, based on his theory of primary property and the science of volition, that appear in this book.

I would like to express my gratitude to Glenn Gardiner, my father, for showing me the bright side; to Andrea Ozment, my editor, for feeling that tickle-up-her-spine; to Richard Warriner for the use of his ear; and to Gloria, my wife, for her love and her laugh.

And to Bob Hudson, Martin Tahse, Sylvia Hirsch, and Ken Gardiner.

Contents

Prologue

No one in the old, run-down house on Felton Street was expecting it.

I know I wasn't. My name's Walter. I was in the dining room playing a game of chess with Major Maddock. We were playing for the usual stakes — my allowance.

Corporal Kimball, I remember, was in the den listening to marching band records, tapping his cane to the beat of the music.

Private Patterson was out on the back porch as usual, asleep in his wheelchair, a book spread open on his lap. He gets a new book every month in the mail, but he never reads them.

My mother was in the kitchen making lunch for everyone. I could hear her opening and closing cupboards.

It was just a typical summer day in that old, run-down house on Felton Street. I guess that's why no one was expecting it . . .

1
The Letter

"Butterfingers!" The Major glared at me with his one good eye. He wore a black patch over the other.

"It was an accident," I said as I reached for the chess piece I had knocked over.

"Must you be so clumsy?"

"Mom says it's just a growing stage. Next year when I'm twelve —"

"I wish you'd hurry up."

"I'm getting better."

"Not much." The Major's good eye looked back to the chessboard.

As the Major studied the board, I studied the Major's eighty-year-old face. I tried to imagine how he must have looked when he was younger, the fearless commando, the leader of the elite rescue force called the Spitzers.

"Check," said the Major.

"What?" And then I saw what had happened. "You tricked me."

"Surprise, my dear boy, is the most important weapon in any battle." He grinned.

I inched my chair forward, accidentally bumping the table. "Sorry." I studied the board. I moved my queen. "This not only eliminates your check, but I now have you in check."

The Major stopped grinning. "Not a bad move."

"Would I make a good commando?" I asked.

"You have the brains for it. Too bad you're so darn uncoordinated."

"If I got coordinated?"

"Perhaps."

"Could I join the Spitzers?"

The Major's black patch moved up and down a few times as if he couldn't control it. He looked at me. "I'm afraid not."

"Why not?"

The Major returned his concentration to the chess-board. "The Spitzers have been disbanded. They existed long ago, before you were born. Far as I know, there are only three of us still living."

"And you all live in this house."

"And we all plan to go on living in this house. No

more fighting for us." The Major moved his bishop between my queen and his own king.

I had anticipated the Major's move. I moved my queen one square to the left. "Check." And then I saw something. "No, I'm sorry. Make that *checkmate*."

"Dad-gum-it! How'd you learn to play like that?"

"You taught me."

"Well, I'm going to stop teaching you." The Major shook his head. "The General warned me to watch out for you."

At the mention of the General, I felt an ache in my chest or my heart or someplace inside me. "I sure miss the General," I said, and as I spoke the old grandfather clock in the living room began to strike twelve. "This house just isn't the same without him."

"We all miss him, Walter. He was quite a man."

"Too bad he had to die."

"Death is something that is kinda hard to avoid."

"The General avoided it once," I said. "When you and the Spitzers saved his life during the war."

"Yes." The Major nodded. "I guess he did."

"You're darn right!" came the loud voice of Corporal Kimball as he hobbled up to the table on his cane. He kicked a chair out with his good leg and sat down. "The way they were torturing him, he wouldn't have lived through the night."

"We were all lucky," said Private Patterson in his soft voice as he powered his wheelchair silently up to the table. He took off the sports cap he always wore and put it on his lap. "We were all lucky we didn't die that day."

I looked at the Major with his black patch and at the Corporal with his cane and at Private Patterson in his wheelchair. All of them were wounded that day they saved the life of General L. R. Britt.

"Walter!" I heard my mother calling from the kitchen. "Is the table set?"

Before I had a chance to answer, the doorbell rang.

"I'll get it," I said, standing up, sending my chair over backward. I took off running for the front door.

"Careful," said my mother, entering the room with a tray full of sandwiches. "You know what happens every time you run."

"Don't worry," I yelled back over my shoulder. As I did, I caught my toe under the rug, which caused me to fall forward, sail through the air, and crash into the screen door, my arm jabbing through it.

I looked up into the surprised face of the mailman, who handed me a special delivery envelope.

After it was determined that I was all right, and after the old-timers had finished laughing, my mother opened the envelope.

Inside was a letter, which she handed to me because she didn't have her glasses.

I read the following aloud so everyone could hear.

> "*Dear Major Maddock, Corporal Kimball, Private Patterson:*
>
> *The purpose of this letter is to inform you that as the sole legal heir to my uncle's estate, I have inherited the house you are living in.*
>
> *My accountants inform me that for many years now my uncle has allowed you to live with him 'rentfree' which also included 'free food' and the services of his housekeeper, Mrs. Wilson.*

As the new owner of the house, I find this arrangement totally unacceptable. Advise Mrs. Wilson that her services are no longer required. As for you three freeloaders who have been sponging off my kindhearted uncle all these years, you have one week to vacate the premises, which means I want you out by next Saturday!

> *— Ralph Britt*
> *Nephew to the late*
> *General L. R. Britt*

P.S. Leave the furniture. I know it's his."

2
The Lawyer

"It's not fair!" I yelled. "The General wanted you guys to have this house."

"Too bad the General forgot to tell his nephew," said Major Maddock as he sat down on the front steps and put his face in his hands.

Corporal Kimball banged his cane down hard on the front porch, said something I'd better not repeat, and then turned and hobbled back into the house and into his room.

Private Patterson didn't say anything. He just looked lost as he began to power his wheelchair from room to room, not exactly sure where to go.

I found my mother in the kitchen. She was crying. She dabbed her eyes with a dishtowel. "What are those poor old men going to do?"

"Don't worry," I told her. "I'll think of something."

Life was like a chess game, the General had always said. For every move there was a countermove. For every strategy, a counterstrategy. Unless, of course, it was checkmate.

Then I noticed the *TV Guide* on the kitchen table. "That's it." I snapped my fingers. "Mr. Hotchkiss, the lawyer who advertises on television. We'll go see him. He'll know what to do."

* * *

Mr. Hotchkiss had an office on the very top floor of the tallest building in town.

His secretary was a tall woman with a pointed nose. She led us into a large, plush office. "Please have a seat." She motioned with her nose toward two comfortable-looking chairs. "Mr. Hotchkiss will be with you momentarily."

"Walter," said my mother as soon as the secretary

had left the office. "You will be careful." She looked around. "You won't touch anything?"

"Mom . . ."

Just then the door opened and Mr. Hotchkiss stormed in. He was an enormous man wearing an enormous dark blue suit that looked more like a tent than a suit.

He took enormous steps as he walked. I counted five long strides from the door to his desk, where he collapsed into his chair. "Good morning," he said, out of breath. He held out an enormous hand. "Let me see the letter."

"Yes, sir," I said, and I handed him Ralph's letter, which he proceeded to read.

Mr. Hotchkiss looked just like he did on TV. Bald head, bug eyes, and a tiny mouth in the shape of a perfect circle. It gave him the appearance of whistling all the time.

"Two questions," said the lawyer when he had finished reading the letter. "One." He held up one finger. "Is Ralph Britt the General's only living relative?"

"I think so." I looked at my mother.

"Yes," she said. "The General had a brother, who was Ralph's father, but he died about a year ago."

"Two." Mr. Hotchkiss held up two fingers. "Did the General leave a will — a Last Will and Testament?"

"Not that I know of." I looked at my mother again. She shook her head.

"Then the house goes to the nephew," said Mr. Hotchkiss. "As well as any other property the General might have had."

"There is a special account at the bank," said my mother. "We use it for groceries and other living expenses."

The lawyer shook his head. "It all belongs to the nephew. Every last cent. That's the law."

And with that, Mr. Hotchkiss stood up and motioned with his hand toward the door. "Thank you for coming in. Please pay my secretary on the way out. And have a nice day."

My mother stood up to leave, but I stayed seated. "What about the General's promise?"

"Now, Walter . . ." said my mother.

"It's all right," said the lawyer, smiling with his little mouth. "I don't mind questions from youngsters. Keeps me on my toes." He looked at me with those bug eyes of his. "What's this about a promise?"

"The General told his buddies that they could go on living in that house for as long as they wanted. He promised them."

"The law does not recognize a promise," said Mr. Hotchkiss, "unless that promise is written down, and then it becomes a will. Without a will, the law clearly states that *all* the deceased's property shall go to the closest living relative — in this case, the General's nephew. Any more questions?"

"But Ralph already has a house," I said. "He lives in a mansion over on Strawberry Hill."

"Ralph could have twenty mansions. That is of no concern to the law."

"What about right and wrong? Isn't the law concerned with that?"

"Of course," said Mr. Hotchkiss. "What's *right* is that Ralph gets the house. It would be *wrong* if he didn't."

"Then the law's *wrong*."

"Walter . . ." said my mother.

"But it is," I insisted. "Ralph didn't even go to the General's funeral."

"That has nothing to do with it," said Mr. Hotchkiss. "The law is the law. Period. We are a country of laws. That is how we live. Without laws there would be utter chaos, disorder. Nothing would be safe."

"I don't see any difference."

"You're talking *anarchy!*" The lawyer pointed his finger at me. "A society without laws." He was getting excited.

My mother took me by the arm and led me over to the door. "Thank you, Mr. Hotchkiss," she said, and then she dragged me out of the office.

But I still had one thing left to say, and I was going to say it. I opened the door back up. "Under this *anarchy*, where there are no laws," I said in a loud voice, "there wouldn't be any lawyers either, would there?"

Mr. Hotchkiss raised both enormous arms in the air, and he opened his tiny mouth as wide as it would open, but he didn't say anything. He just got as red as a beet.

I closed the door quickly. I thought he was going to explode.

On the way home in the taxi, did I ever get it from my mother. She lectured me up one side and down the other about being so rude. "You never talk to an adult that way," she scolded me. "Especially a professional man like Mr. Hotchkiss."

"But Mom," I protested. "We paid Mr. Hotchkiss money to help *us,* and then he turned out to be on Ralph's side."

"I'm sure Mr. Hotchkiss would have done something if he could have."

"A lot of good that does," I said. "So what are we going to tell the vets?"

"The truth," said my mother.

"Which is?"

"That I must find another job, and that they must go back to the army hospital."

"But they hate it there, Mom. They said they'd rather die than go back."

"I know, son. I wish there was something else we could do."

"There is," I said. "I just haven't thought of it yet."

3
Ralph

It wasn't until next morning, just as we were finishing breakfast, that I figured out what my next move was going to be.

"I'm going to go see Ralph," I told the others. "I'm going to have a talk with him."

"Won't do any good," said the Major. "Ralph's a bad seed. As bad as they come."

"His own father couldn't stand him," said the Corporal.

"A boy raised without love," said Private Patterson.

"I think the men are right," said my mother as she began to pick up dishes from the table. "Even our beloved General didn't see any hope when it came to his nephew Ralph."

"Does anyone have a better idea?" I said. No one did. "Then I'm going to go see him."

After the dishes were done, I got on my bike and rode over to Strawberry Hill, which was way on the other side of town.

Ralph lived in a mansion surrounded by a high stone wall. The only way into the place was through locked iron gates that blocked the driveway.

I pressed the buzzer on the intercom box to announce my arrival. I had been over to the mansion before with the General to visit Ralph's father, but I had never actually met Ralph. I wondered if he was really as bad as everyone said.

"Who is it?" came the sound of a voice over the intercom.

"My name's Walter Wilson," I said. "I would like to —"

"If you're selling magazines, I don't read. If you're selling light bulbs, I go to bed early. If you're selling anything else, I don't need it. If I do need it, I've already bought it."

"I'm not selling anything."

"I don't give donations. I don't believe in charity. Not one cent."

"I'm not here to ask you for money."

"Then what do you want?"

"I just want to talk."

"Talk? Talk about what?"

"The house on Felton Street."

There was a long pause. "What do you know about the house on Felton Street?"

"Lots of things. What would you like to know?"

There was another long pause. "Is my newspaper down there?"

I looked around. The newspaper was in the driveway. "Yes, it is."

"I'll be down in a minute."

Almost immediately the front door of the mansion opened, and out walked a tall, sticklike man dressed in his pajamas and bathrobe. He shuffled along in his slippers as he made his way down the long driveway from the mansion to the front gate.

The closer he got, the uglier he got. His face looked like a skull with a thin layer of skin stretched over it. I found myself backing up as he approached the gate.

"Give me my newspaper," he ordered. I handed it to him through the bars. He proceeded to thumb through the newspaper for a while, and then he asked, "What about the house on Felton Street?"

"I live there," I said. "My mother and I take care of the General's three army buddies."

Ralph looked at me with his bloodshot eyes. "At my expense. I'll be paying the bills, you know. Do you have any idea how much you people are going to cost me?"

"No, I don't. But we're worth it. We take real good care of the men. Mom's a good cook, and she doesn't buy the most expensive, except maybe for the Corporal's birthday last month when we splurged and had roast duck."

"You people are eating duck?"

"I work around the house, pulling weeds and watering —"

"And what do I get out of all this?"

"What do you mean?"

"I pay out money. What do I get back in return?"

"You get . . . nothing."

"Precisely," said Ralph, jerking his head. "You look like a smart boy. Would you call our little arrangement a smart thing to do with *my* money?"

"It's what the General wanted done with *his* money, not *your* money."

"What the General chose to do with his money was his business. Now that his money belongs to me, it's my business, and I want those bums out of my house."

"They're not bums."

"Anyone who doesn't pay his own way is a bum."

"They paid, back during the war when they saved the General's life. Now the General is paying them back."

"They've been paid back. The General has been supporting them for years."

"The General promised to take care of them *forever*."

"When the General died, all his promises died with him." Ralph began to thumb through his newspaper again, and then he said in a low voice, "If those old geezers meant so much to the General, why didn't he leave a will?"

"I don't know. Maybe he figured because you had this mansion, you wouldn't want that old house."

"He figured wrong, didn't he?" Ralph grinned, stretching the skin on his face even tighter.

"I guess they were right about you," I said. "I kept hoping you'd be like your father. He was real nice to us. He used to invite us over here for birthdays and Thanksgiving. Which reminds me, how come we never met you?"

"Because . . ." Ralph began to chew his lower lip. "I was never invited. My father and I didn't get along."

"I heard he gave you anything you wanted."

"On one condition — that I *never* come around."

"He paid you to stay away?"

Ralph nodded, looking at the ground. I suddenly felt sorry for him.

"How would you like to come over to our house for dinner?"

"Me?" Ralph blinked his eyes, and I think he tried to smile.

"Yes," I said. "I'm inviting you."

"Why would you want to do that?"

"Because Mom's a great cook, and afterward you could play a game of chess with the Major or listen to some of the Corporal's records or borrow a book from Private Patterson."

Ralph seemed to consider the invitation for a moment, and then he said, "You can't fool me. I see what you're trying to do. I wasn't born yesterday."

"I wasn't trying to —"

"I want you out of that house!" He began shuffling backward up the driveway. "I'm warning you. If you're not out by Saturday, I'll have you thrown out."

4
The Hospital

The next morning after breakfast, a taxi arrived outside the old, run-down house on Felton Street.

"Seems we could have waited till Saturday," said the Major.

"I'm not going!" said the Corporal.

"Do we have to?" said Private Patterson.

"You'll be coming right back," I said. "You guys just have to sign some papers, that's all."

Reluctantly, the men agreed. The cab driver and I helped them into the back seat. We put Private Patterson's wheelchair into the trunk. Mom couldn't come with us because she had a job interview.

"Veterans' Hospital," I said to the driver, who squealed the tires as we drove off.

The Veterans' Hospital was a special hospital to take care of people who had fought in the war — any war, I guess, just as long as you were on our side. The hospital was located in the center of town. It used to be an old hotel. It was not a very pretty sight, and to make matters worse, it was a cloudy day, which just made the place look all the more depressing.

I told the driver to stop next to a concrete ramp that led up to the main entrance.

"We used to rescue people from better looking places than this," said the Major as he eased himself out of the car.

"Rat-tat-tat-tat," went Corporal Kimball, aiming his cane at the building.

Private Patterson just yawned as I pushed him up the ramp, following the others into the mouth of the cold, dark building.

"What's that smell?" I asked the moment we were inside.

"Hospital," said the Major.

"Old people," said Private Patterson.

"*Death,*" said Corporal Kimball.

The admissions office was on the first floor. I found it easily. Inside was a woman clerk with short hair and husky shoulders seated at a desk playing cards with herself.

"Excuse me," I said.

"Just a moment," said the clerk in a low voice, continuing to turn over cards three at a time. She must have lost, because suddenly she stood up and threw the cards down on the desk. She looked at us. "What do you want?"

"My friends have to sign some papers?"

"Coming or going?"

"Admissions papers," I said.

The woman reached into a drawer and took out some forms. She sat back down at her desk and put one of the forms into a typewriter. She proceeded to ask a whole lot of questions in a very loud voice.

"Name! Rank! Serial number!"

Each of the vets, especially the Corporal, answered her questions in a *very* loud voice. This just made the clerk talk all the louder, which in turn made the vets talk all the louder, until they were all shouting at each other.

"Date of arrival!" The woman's powerful voice rang out in the small room.

Silence. This was one question the vets didn't feel like shouting about.

"Saturday," I said. "But they can change their minds, right?"

"Sure." The clerk shrugged her husky shoulders. "If you can find somebody who wants them." She flashed the vets a phony smile. "A bus will be by to pick you guys up Saturday afternoon."

"Not if we can help it," said the Major.

"I'd rather die," said the Corporal.

"I want to see my room," said Private Patterson.

"Is it all right?" I asked the clerk.

"Ninth floor," she said. "Ask for *the ward*."

The ward turned out to be one large room with a hundred beds in it — all of them taken.

"Where are they going to put you guys?" I asked as we made our way down an aisle between rows of occupied beds.

"People drop like flies around this place," said Corporal Kimball. "Should be plenty of beds by Saturday."

I tried not to stare as we passed the beds, even though I could tell that the people in those beds were looking at us. I tried to imagine how these men must have looked in their uniforms, how proud they must have been. I wondered if anyone ever thought of making uniformed pajamas.

We were about halfway down the aisle when voices rang out.

"It's Major Maddock!"

"The Spitzers are here!"

"They've come to rescue us!"

All around us men stood up beside their beds and saluted. Those who couldn't stand, sat up and saluted. Those who couldn't sit up, saluted from a lying down position.

The Major returned their salutes. So did Corporal Kimball and Private Patterson. Someone started cheering. Others joined in. Pillows were thrown into the air as people rushed forward, shaking our hands, patting us on the back, until we were completely surrounded by cheering, smiling faces. Everyone had heard of the Spitzers. They were a legend.

"You *have* come to get us out of here?" a one-armed man asked the Major. The man's face was filled with hope.

The room became deathly quiet. All eyes were on the Major, including mine.

"You certainly didn't come to join us," said the one-armed man, laughing. Everyone laughed. Everyone except the Spitzers and me.

"I did *not* come here to rescue you," said the Major.

"Then why are you here?" said the one-armed man.

"I'm here because —"

"Because . . ." I interrupted. "The Major wanted me to meet the men he fought with. I'm glad to make your acquaintance."

My statement caused more cheering, and then someone started singing a song, and everyone joined in. After the singing came the stories. "Did the Major ever tell you about the time . . ."

We spent the rest of the morning listening to old war stories. Some of the stories were funny, and we all laughed. Some of the stories were not funny, like when someone's friend was killed, and we all got real sad. Some of the men even cried. Old people aren't ashamed to cry.

A bottle of something called "rotgut" was passed around. I took a swig and sprayed it right out. Everyone seemed to think it was real funny. I didn't. The stuff tasted like gasoline.

One of the men showed me a coin that he wore around his neck. It had a big dent in it. "Saved my life," he said. "Just as sure as I'm standing here."

"That's it," I whispered to myself as I looked at the coin. I didn't tell the others, but right then and there I knew everything was going to be all right.

5
The Bank

"You should have let me tell them," said the Major as we left the hospital. "What are they going to think when we come back here on Saturday to stay?"

"That's just it," I said. "You guys are never coming back here."

"What do you mean?" The Major stopped at the top of the ramp.

"It was the coin." I brought Private Patterson's wheelchair to a stop. "The one that saved the man's life. It reminded me of the General's coin collection."

"So?" said the Corporal. "How's a coin collection going to help us?"

"The General used to keep his coin collection in his safe-deposit box at the bank." I held onto the wheelchair with one hand and pointed to a tall building a couple of blocks away. "That building right over there."

"Go on, Walter," said the Major.

"The General promised you the house, but he wouldn't have left it at that. You knew the General. He was always so careful, left nothing to chance, always had a *back-up*."

"That's right," said the Corporal.

"What are you trying to say, Walter?"

"I'm convinced the General left a will — a Last Will and Testament — and I'll bet you my allowance it's in his safe-deposit box at the bank. It's the most logical place."

"Right under our noses," said the Corporal, looking over at the bank building.

"Good thinking, Walter," said the Major. "I always said you had the brains." He stuck out his hand.

"Thank you, sir." I let go of Private Patterson's wheelchair and shook the Major's hand.

When I turned around again, the wheelchair wasn't there. It was rolling down the ramp and picking up speed.

"Oh, no!" I took off running, my tennis shoes slipping on the concrete as I tried to get some traction. As I ran down the ramp, I could see Private Patterson's sports cap bobbing up and down in front of me. I could also see a parked car at the bottom of the ramp which Private Patterson was sure to smash into unless I could catch him.

I was gaining on him. I was almost there. I realized I wasn't going to make it. I dove or tripped (I'm not sure which), hit the concrete, and grabbed the back of the wheelchair, bringing it to a stop just inches from the parked car.

"Must you be so jerky?" said Private Patterson in a sleepy voice.

"Sorry, sir. It won't happen again."

I had skinned my elbow, but I didn't say anything. I was more mad than hurt. Private Patterson had survived the war — several wars — but would he survive me? I guess the Major was right. I wasn't ready to be a Spitzer. Not yet, anyway.

It took twenty minutes to go the two blocks from the hospital to the bank building. Old people just don't go very fast. At one intersection, the light turned before we got across, and a car started honking. The Corporal hit the bumper of the car with his cane. The honking stopped.

The bank was nice and cool inside. I guided the three men over to some soft-looking couches and told them to wait for me. Private Patterson insisted on looking at a brochure. I gave him one even though I knew he would just fall asleep, which he did.

I walked past a long line of customers over to a small desk to the right of the teller windows. I could see the open vault fifteen feet away and the safe-deposit boxes inside. The will was there. I could feel it.

"May I help you?" said a gray-haired lady, walking up to the desk. She seemed real nice.

"Yes," I said, wondering what I was going to say. "You see, my friends and I are looking for something, and we think it might be in our safe-deposit box. It will just take a second to look."

"Have you filled out a form?"

"Form?" That's right. The General always filled out one of those yellow forms that were on the desk.

"Here you are." The lady handed me one. "I'll be right back."

I sat down at the desk and studied the form. Where it said *Name*, I wrote GENERAL L. R. BRITT. Where it said *Box number*, I didn't know what to do. I couldn't remember the number. I thought it started with a two . . .

I stood up and looked into the vault. All the safe-deposit boxes I could see had three numbers. I decided to guess, but before I could write anything, the gray-haired lady returned.

"I'll take that." She held out her hand. I handed her the form. She looked at me with a puzzled expression. "You've forgotten to write down your box number."

"I can't remember it."

"It's on your key."

"Key?" How could I be so dumb? The General had a key, and so did the bank. It took two keys to open a safe-deposit box.

The woman glanced at the form one more time. She tilted her head to the side. "You're a little young to be a general, aren't you?"

"Yes, ma'am." I decided to tell her everything. All about the General and the vets and the old house on Felton Street, and about Ralph and the hospital and the coin that saved the man's life, and, of course, about the will. "So, you see, I don't *want* what's in the box, I just want to *know* what's in it."

"The contents of a safe-deposit box are confidential," said the lady, tearing up the little slip I had given her. "General Britt didn't have to tell us what he put in it, and I certainly don't have to tell you." She put the pieces in the trash can under the desk. "Furthermore, when a person dies, his safe-deposit box is sealed until his estate

is settled, so I couldn't tell you even if I wanted to, which I don't."

"What if no one knew the box was here? What if the General kept it a secret? Then it would still be here, right?"

"I guess it would be, but I still —"

"All I want to know is if the General still has a box here. Can you at least tell me that? It's real important to those three gentlemen over there on the couch. You don't know how important." I looked over toward the couch, which was a mistake because all three of the vets were asleep.

"It's highly irregular," said the gray-haired lady, "but I guess it won't hurt anything."

She went over to a file cabinet and came back with a

card. "According to this, the General's box was closed out on the sixteenth of last month."

"That's impossible. That was the day the General died."

"Are you saying someone forged the General's signature?"

"Yes. And I know exactly who it was."

6
The Tape

"Ralph stole the will," I told my mother when we got home.

"What will?"

"The one we *think* the General wrote," said the Major.

"I'm sure he wrote it," I said, and I proceeded to tell my mother the whole story.

"So what can we do?"

"Not much," said the Major. "Even if there was a will, Ralph has certainly destroyed it by now."

The others agreed. Without a will there wasn't too much we could do.

"I'm afraid I have some more bad news," said my mother. "I've found a new job. I start tomorrow. Walter will stay here and take care of you until Saturday."

"Oh, no," said the Corporal. "Remember the last time Butterfingers tried to cook?"

That night Mom prepared roast duck for a farewell dinner. It was the best she'd ever cooked, but no one seemed to notice.

After dinner, I helped my mother pack her things, and the following morning I called for a taxi.

"I'll come by the hospital and visit you," she told the vets, and then she started to kiss them and cry and blow her nose, all at the same time. She waved her handkerchief out the window as the taxi drove off.

"How dare Ralph break up our family?" said the Major as we watched the taxi disappear down at the end of Felton Street.

"I say we tar and feather him," said the Corporal.

"Make him cry uncle," said Private Patterson.

"That's it!" I said. "What if we get Ralph to *admit* he stole the will?"

"You mean a confession?" said the Major.

"Yes."

The Major rubbed his chin and squinted his good eye. "A confession plus the forgery at the bank should be enough to nail him."

"But how are we going to get him to confess?" said Private Patterson.

"Leave him to me." The Corporal gripped his cane so hard that his knuckles turned white.

"I have an easier way." I raced into the house and came back with the small tape recorder the vets had given me for my birthday last year. "I'll get Ralph to admit it on tape."

"That may be easier said than done." The Major and the others didn't seem too enthusiastic about my idea.

"Don't worry," I told them. "You just leave everything to me."

Since Ralph knew what I looked like, I needed a disguise. I found some dark glasses and an old wig of my mother's that I had used for a Halloween costume.

Next, I had to figure out a way to get past those locked gates at the mansion. Once inside, I was sure I could get Ralph to talk about the will. The solution came to me when I noticed a nickel and some pennies on the dresser. *"Money,"* I said out loud. The one word that would get Ralph to open those gates. I was ready.

To announce my departure, I decided to play "Charge" on the Spitzer bugle, which was kept behind glass doors in a cabinet in the hallway. I wasn't allowed to touch the bugle without permission, but under the circumstances I figured it would be all right.

"Walter," came the sound of the Major's voice as I was putting the bugle to my lips. "Put that bugle down. You know only a Spitzer is allowed to touch it."

"I'm sorry." I put the bugle back into the cabinet. "I just thought —"

"I'm sorry, too," said the Major. "Sorry to yell at you. I know you were just trying to cheer us up."

"I'm going to do more than try." I opened the front

door. "When I come back, I'm going to have Ralph's confession."

I bicycled over to Strawberry Hill in record time, my disguise stuffed under my shirt, my tape recorder in my jacket pocket.

"Who is it?" said Ralph's voice over the intercom.

"Delivery from City Bank."

There was a long pause. "What are you delivering?"

"Money."

"Money?"

"Coins, actually. Part of General Britt's *coin collection*."

A buzzer sounded. I pushed opened the heavy iron gates. I was inside. I quickly slipped on the wig and dark glasses. I pressed the PLAY and RECORD buttons on the tape recorder. "Testing. Testing." The indicator light flashed, showing that it was picking up my voice. Everything was set.

"Would you hurry up?" came the sound of Ralph's voice, and I looked up to see Ralph standing on the front porch of the mansion. He was dressed as before, in his bathrobe and pajamas.

I slipped the tape recorder into my jacket pocket as I walked slowly up the long driveway to the mansion.

"I don't have all day, you know," said Ralph in a disgusted tone of voice. He held out his hand. "Let me see the coins."

"Are you Ralph Britt?" I said it loudly so the tape would be sure to pick it up.

"Yes. Yes." He jerked his hand. "Give them to me."

"I'm sorry," I said. "I must see some identification." I faked a smile. "Bank rules."

"Ridiculous." Ralph motioned for me to follow him inside. "Such an inconvenience. Now I must find my wallet."

The inside of the mansion was a mess. The floor was so dirty that I could hear my own footsteps as we walked. Piles of magazines and newspapers were all over the place, and I even saw cobwebs in the chandeliers. But what got me the most was the smell, which was a combination of dust, cigarettes, and popcorn all mixed together.

"This way. This way." Ralph led me into the living room where he had *three* of those big screen televisions — all on, each on a different station. In front of the couch were two bowls as big as fish tanks. One was filled with popcorn, the other with cigarette butts. I'm not kidding.

"Here it is," said Ralph, holding up his driver's license for me to see. He held out his other hand. "Give me the coins."

"Just one more question," I said, although I wasn't exactly sure what I was going to say. "Do you have . . . the rest of the General's coin collection?"

"Of course I have it."

"The collection that was in the General's safe-deposit box?"

"Yes. Yes." He held out his hand, moving his finger tips.

"General Britt's safe-deposit box at City Bank that also contained the General's Last Will and Testament?"

"Say, who are you?" Ralph seemed to notice my disguise for the first time.

"Then there was a will?"

"I recognize your voice," said Ralph. "You're the boy who was here yesterday."

"You took the will, didn't you?" I said. "On the sixteenth of last month. The day the General died. You forged the General's signature, and then you took what was in the box, which included the General's coin collection and his will leaving the old house on Felton Street to his friends."

"You know about that?" Ralph seemed stunned.

"Then you admit it. There was a will?"

"You're not sure?" Ralph's expression changed from stunned to confused. Then he seemed to return to his normal self. "Yes, there *was* a will, but I destroyed it, so you can't prove a thing."

"Thank you," I said. "That's just what I wanted to hear." I turned and ran, the tape recorder clutched tightly in my hand.

7
The Search

"I've got it!" I ran into the house, holding the tape recorder in the air. "It's all on tape."

"Mission successful," said the Major.

"Way to go, Walter," said Private Patterson.

"Nothing went wrong?" said the Corporal.

"Everything went perfect. I got Ralph to admit that he took the will and that he destroyed it. Everything." I shook the tape recorder. "It's all right here."

"Walter," said the Major, and he sounded very serious.

"Did I do something wrong?"

"No." The Major removed a small black box from his pocket. "You did nothing wrong." He handed me the box. "This is for you."

I opened the box. Inside was something I recognized immediately. It was a Spitzer medal — a jagged piece

of lightning being extinguished by a big glob of spit.

"You mean I'm a Spitzer now?"

"An honorary one," said the Major, "but a Spitzer just the same."

"Thank you." I couldn't take my eyes off the medal.

"You earned it, Walter. Now, let's listen to that tape."

I stuffed the medal into my pocket and laid the tape recorder on the table. "I'll have to rewind it first."

"You haven't listened to it?" said the Corporal.

"I was in too much of a hurry to get home." I pressed the REWIND button. Nothing happened. I pressed it again. Still nothing. "What's going on?" I banged the recorder on the table.

"Batteries," said the Major. "Do you have any others?"

"My radio uses the same size." I went to my room and got my transistor radio. I switched batteries and pressed the REWIND button again. It worked. "Whew," I said. When it stopped rewinding, I pressed the PLAY button, and in a short time I heard the sound of my own voice saying, "Are you Ralph Britt?"

"That's where I started," I said.

"I'm more concerned with where you ended," said the Major.

We listened to some more, and then all of a sudden the voices started speeding up.

"What's happening?" I asked.

"The old batteries are dying," explained the Major. "It recorded slower, so when it's played back it sounds faster."

And then there was nothing. "The batteries died, didn't they?" I said.

"I'm afraid so, Walter."

"Just as Ralph was spilling the beans." Corporal Kimball banged his cane on the floor.

"That's too bad," said Private Patterson.

"I blew it. The tape's worthless." I took the Spitzer medal out of my pocket and put it on the table. "I don't deserve this."

I went to my room and closed the door. I proceeded to punch my pillow. Once! Twice! After four or five punches, I heard a knock. "Walter?" It was the Major's voice. "May we come in?"

"I guess so." I punched my pillow one more time.

The door opened and Major Maddock walked in, followed by Corporal Kimball hobbling on his cane and Private Patterson in his wheelchair. They all crammed into my small room.

"I'm going to tell you something, Walter," said the Major, "and I want you to listen good." He waited until I nodded my head before he went on. "When I gave you that medal, you became a *Spitzer,* and a Spitzer never quits. He never gives up. Do you understand?"

"I understand."

"Good." The Major handed me the Spitzer medal I had left on the table. "This belongs to you."

"Thank you," I said, taking the medal. "I just feel so stupid. I should have had a back-up. If there was one thing the General taught me, it was always to have a back-up."

The word *back-up* stuck in my throat like a chicken bone. The General never went anyplace without two of everything — two thermos bottles, two flashlights, two . . ."

"Wills."

"What's that?" said the Major.

"All this time I thought the will in the safe-deposit box was the back-up for the General's promise, but what if I was wrong? That would mean there must be a back-up will for the original will."

"Two wills?"

"A copy," I said. "Hidden somewhere where you guys would be sure to find it." I thought for a moment. "The most logical place is . . ."

"This *house!*" We all seemed to say it at once.

The search for the missing copy of the will began.

I helped the Major look through the General's old foot locker that was stored in the attic. It was mostly filled with old clothes and old photographs. We checked every shirt pocket and every pants pocket and between the pages of every photo album, and every other place we could think of.

Corporal Kimball and I went over every inch of the

General's old room. We checked under the rug and under the mattress and under the drawers in the chest of drawers and even behind the mirror.

I helped Private Patterson check the downstairs. We checked behind the cushions on the sofa and inside the cushions that had zippers and in the cupboards in the kitchen and behind the stove and in all the cracks and crannies and all the other hard to reach places we could think of.

And the search did not end that day, or that night, or the next day. We continued to search every square inch of that old, run-down house on Felton Street, stopping only for short periods to rest or to eat tuna fish sandwiches with onions and pickle relish, the only thing I knew how to make that the vets would eat.

We even searched outside the house. We searched the front porch and the back porch, the front yard and the back yard, the bushes and the trees, the flowers and the weeds. I even climbed onto the roof and checked the chimney. Until finally there were no more places to look.

I then had to say something that was very difficult for me to say, but I knew I had to say it. "I'll help you pack. The bus will be here tomorrow."

8
Saturday

The next day was Saturday. We were awakened at six in the morning by a loud knock at the door.

It was the movers. They had come for the furniture. There were two men. One was tall and the other short. Both were wearing white overalls. They parked their large, white moving van on the front lawn.

I moved the vets and their stuff — one suitcase each and some cardboard boxes — out onto the front porch so we'd be out of their way.

We watched as the two men proceeded to empty the house of all its furniture. It was real sad to see the dining room table being taken away. I had played a lot of games of chess on that table, not to mention all the neat stories I had listened to after dinner.

"Wait a minute," I called out when I saw the two

men carrying out the chest with the glass doors that had been in the hallway.

The men stopped. "This belongs to us." I opened the glass doors and removed the Spitzer bugle.

In a very short time the house was completely cleaned out — furniture, rugs, lighting fixtures. Even some of the nicer windows had been removed.

We watched as the truck drove off, taking with it a part of our lives.

The next thing we knew, a long, black Cadillac — badly in need of a wash — pulled into our driveway and stopped in front of the garage. Right behind it was a pickup truck which had some company name printed on the side.

Ralph Britt got out of the Cadillac. He looked almost normal — his hair was combed, and he was wearing regular clothes.

A fat man in a T-shirt with tattoos on his arms and a cigar butt between his teeth got out of the pickup.

Ralph and the fat man started talking, pointing at the house.

"Is that who I think it is?" said Corporal Kimball.

"In the flesh," I said.

"Wonder what he wants?" said Private Patterson.

"Come to gloat," said the Major. "It's like him."

Before I realized it, the Corporal had hobbled down the steps and was making his way across the front lawn toward Ralph and the fat man.

"Corporal Kimball!" I shouted, trying to stand up, but I had caught my tennis shoe in a crack on the steps.

"Swine," said the Corporal, and he swung his cane at Ralph.

"Get away from me," said Ralph, running behind the fat man for protection.

"Not till I teach you a lesson." Corporal Kimball swung his cane again.

The fat man reached out with one of his tattooed arms and grabbed the cane. With a flick of the wrist, he jerked the cane away from the Corporal. "Just think, old man, this could be you," he said as he brought the cane down over his knee, breaking it in two.

I ran over and picked up the broken cane and then helped the Corporal back to the porch.

"I'm not afraid of him."

"I know you're not."

"Same old Kimball," said the Major, shaking his head. "All brawn and no brains."

"Least I did something," said the Corporal, collapsing onto the steps.

"You almost had him," said Private Patterson.

"Walter," said the Major, straining to see with his good eye. "What's that say on the side of the pickup?"

"Ace . . ." I had to step to the side to see around Ralph who was standing in front of the pickup. "Ace Demolition." I looked at the Major. "Does that mean what I think it means?"

"Yes, Walter. That's exactly what it means."

I got so mad, I stormed across the front lawn. The fat man had gotten into his pickup and had started the engine. As I approached, I heard Ralph say to him, "I want you here at six in the morning, sharp."

"I'll be here," said the fat man. "And so will *Betsy*. Won't take us more than ten minutes to level this baby."

He chuckled as he backed his pickup out of the driveway.

"Betsy's a wrecking ball, isn't it?" I said to Ralph, who spun around, startled at the sound of my voice. He looked relieved when he saw it was only me.

"If it isn't the delivery boy from the bank." He stood up tall and looked down at me.

"You're going to smash this house down, aren't you?"

"It's my house." He shrugged. "I'll do what I want."

"Not if the General was around, you wouldn't."

"But he's not, is he?"

"I know why you want to destroy this house. You know about the missing copy of the will. You know it's hidden somewhere in the house, but you don't know where, so you're going to make sure nobody ever finds it."

"Smart boy."

"Smart enough to figure you out."

"But not smart enough to stop me." Ralph grinned, and when he did, I wanted to hurt him.

"The General didn't love you," I said, and I could tell by the look on Ralph's face that my comment hurt. "You were his nephew, and he didn't love you, and I can see why."

"The *General*." Ralph spit out the word. "He was such a big war hero. How do you impress a big war hero? Huh, smart boy?"

He waited for me to say something, but I didn't say anything, so he kept talking. "I got in a fight once, right in front of him. I thought that would do it, but it didn't. He just called me a coward."

"What did you do, run?"

"Heck, no. I beat her up."

"Did you say *her?* You beat up a girl?"

"She was taller than I was."

I was so flabbergasted that I didn't know what to say, so I just stood there and watched as Ralph got into his car. He rolled down the window so he could say something. "Nice knowing you, smart boy." He started the engine. "Say good-by to the old geezers for me."

As he drove off, I could hear him laughing and coughing — coughing the way people who smoke a lot do.

9
Good-by

I looked at my watch. The bus was due any minute, and when it came, I would have to say good-by to my best friends.

"Walter," said the Major as we sat on the steps of the front porch. "I want you to have this." He handed me a shoebox.

"This is your chess set," I said, recognizing the box. "I can't take this."

"You'll get more use out of it than I will."

"But you'll have plenty of time to play at the hospital."

"I don't feel much like playing anymore."

"Do you really want me to have it?" I touched the pieces, which were made of real brass.

"Yes, Walter. I do."

"I'll never forget what you taught me, and all the great games we had."

"Nor will I."

"Do you want to play a quick game before the bus gets here?"

The Major shook his head and looked away.

"Butterfingers." It was the Corporal's turn. "See that box over there?" He pointed with his broken cane, which I had taped together with some extra tape we had left over from packing. "Those are my records. Best marching band music you'll ever hear." He looked at me. "They're yours."

"You can listen to your records at the hospital."

"I don't have a phonograph. It belonged to the General."

"But surely the hospital will have a phonograph."

"Even if they do . . ." He rattled his cane. "What's the use of listening to music in a place like that?"

Before I could say anything, Private Patterson spoke up. "It would make me very happy if you would take my books." He smiled at me with those sleepy eyes of his. "I have some nice ones."

"I know you do, but . . ." And then I remembered that Private Patterson never read them, anyway. All he needed was any old magazine on his lap to make him fall asleep. "Thank you," I said. "Thanks, all of you. I'll take real good care of your stuff. I promise."

Just then we heard something, and we all turned and looked down the street. It was a taxi. The taxi stopped in front of the house and Mom got out. She could only stay a minute because the new place she was working at was real strict, and she had to get right back.

"You'll be fine," she told the vets, but I could tell from the sound of her voice that she didn't believe it. She kissed each of them on the forehead, gave them each a hug, and then got back in the taxi and left, her handkerchief waving out the window.

The bus arrived. It was a big, green army bus. It was empty except for the bus driver, a young man who chewed gum with his mouth open.

"Maddock," he called out, chewing as he talked. "Kimball. Patterson."

"It's *Major* Maddock," I said. *"Corporal* Kimball. *Private* Patterson."

"Anything you say, kid." He chewed a little faster. "Is that their stuff?" He pointed to their things on the front porch.

"Just the suitcases and those boxes," I said. "The rest of the stuff stays."

As the driver began to load the suitcases onto the bus, I turned to my friends.

"Good-by, Major." I shook the Major's hand.

"Good-by." I shook Corporal Kimball's hand.

"Good-by, Private Patterson."

"Good-by, Walter."

We stood there for a moment looking at each other, and then I found myself hugging each one of them and crying like a baby. I'm not ashamed of it, either.

"Straighten up, Butterfingers," said the Corporal.

But I could tell he was crying, too.

"It's all right," said Private Patterson. "We're used to being casualties."

"Walter," said the Major. "I want you to tell your mother something for me."

"What's that, sir?"

"I want you to tell her that she has a fine son, a real Spitzer if I ever saw one."

"Do you mean it?"

"I don't say things I don't mean."

"I'm going to miss you," I said.

A tear appeared in the Major's good eye and rolled down his cheek. He gave my hand a squeeze, and then he turned and got onto the bus. The others followed. I helped the driver with Private Patterson.

I stood on the sidewalk staring up at them. They had their heads pressed up against the bus windows, staring down at me. Major Maddock, Corporal Kimball, Private Patterson. The Spitzers, who had rescued so many, and now, when they were in need . . .

The driver started the engine. Private Patterson started to wave.

I calmly walked over and stood in front of the bus, holding out my arms.

"What are you doing, kid?" said the driver, sticking his gum-chewing head out the window.

"Tell them to get off."

That's all I said, but I must have sounded like I meant it, because in less than five minutes the bus was gone and there on the sidewalk were the vets and their luggage. No one said anything. They were waiting for me to speak.

"When I tried to give this back to you," I said, holding up my Spitzer medal, "you wouldn't let me. You told me that a Spitzer never quits. So we're not quitting."

"What do you suggest we do, Walter?" said the Major.

"*Fight,*" I said, and the calmness with which I said it surprised me. "We're not giving up this house without a fight."

10
The General

The dining room was officially renamed the war room. I dragged in some old lawn chairs from the garage, which was filled with junk the movers had left behind. I also found an old door which I converted into a table by laying it on some orange crates.

With a Magic Marker, I began to draw on the door. I sketched an aerial view of the house, now referred to as "the compound." I sketched the grounds around the house and the road in front, the big maple tree, the lawn area leading up to the house, and the driveway going to the garage.

"This is how I figure it," I said to the others. "They'll get here about six in the morning. They'll bring the wrecking ball in from the main road and set it up approximately here." I drew a large X on the door.

"If we just had a bazooka," said the Corporal, banging his cane in the usual manner.

"How about a tank?" said Private Patterson.

"Quiet, you two," said the Major. "This is a briefing."

"We don't have a bazooka," I told the Corporal, "but we do have a hose."

"A hose?" said the Corporal. "Blast them with water?"

"And we do have a tank." I looked at Private Patterson.

"We do?" The Private tilted back his sports cap.

I drew a quick sketch on the door.

"Those look like trash cans," said the Private.

"They are," I said. "The ones on the side of the house. They're metal and real strong. If we put one on the front and the other on the back, so they face each other as I've shown here, and put the lids on the sides, and fix a toilet seat in between to allow a person to poke his head up and look around — we have a *tank*."

"What about power?" said the Major. "How will the tank move?"

"We have power." I looked at Private Patterson. "Wheelchair power. We'll build the tank around Private Patterson's wheelchair."

The Private smiled.

"Wait a darn minute," said Corporal Kimball. "You don't expect us to go up against a wrecking ball with a garden hose and a wheelchair?"

"Yes," I said. "I've got it all worked out."

The Corporal looked at the Major.

"If that's all we have," said the Major, "then, by

golly, that's what we'll use. Now, keep quiet, and let's hear what the boy has to say."

Corporal Kimball grumbled, mumbling something under his breath about an air strike.

I proceeded to tell them about my plan. I talked slowly and carefully so that they would be sure to understand, because each of them had something important to do. "Any questions?"

There were no questions, only smiles.

"It just might work," said the Corporal.

"Brilliant strategy," said the Major. "How did you think of it?"

"You always told me that *surprise* was the most important weapon in any battle. So, since we don't have any real weapons, I just figured we better have a lot of surprises."

"Good thinking," said the Major. "I'm impressed."

Almost everything I needed for my plan, including an old gasoline can, I was able to find in the garage. For the other things, I rode my bicycle to the supermarket. Besides some food, I bought a package of balloons, two black squirt guns, and a cigarette lighter. I made sure the lighter had plenty of fluid. I wasn't going to make that mistake again.

When I returned home, it was just getting dark. I found the vets hard at work. Major Maddock was busy repairing the hose, which had more than a couple of

holes in it. Corporal Kimball was in the process of lug-
ging several old paint cans from the garage up to the
roof. Private Patterson was whistling as he cleaned the
trash cans. "Gonna be a fine tank," he said, and then
he went on whistling and scrubbing.

I stuffed the package of balloons into my pocket and
started to run up the stairs, slipped, but caught myself.
"Careful," I told myself. "I must be careful."

For the next half hour, I helped the Corporal fill about
twenty balloons with paint. We would have filled more,
but we ran out of paint.

I went back down the stairs and inspected the Major's
patch job on the hose. "Looks good." I dragged the hose
into the living room. I opened the front window a few
inches. I made sure the nozzle on the end of the hose
was in the off position, and then I fixed the hose in place
by poking it through the screen.

The tank was next. With some wire and some rope I
found in the garage, I was able to fix one trash can to
the front of the wheelchair and the other to the back.
The trash can lids went on the sides, the toilet seat in
between, and I found an old bucket Private Patterson
could use as a helmet.

"That's it," I said, walking back into the house.
"We're ready." And then I saw the worried look on
the Major's face. "What's wrong?"

"Communications," said the Major. "This operation

must be coordinated, but I see no way to do it without a radio."

"Too late to pick up a walkie-talkie," I said, looking at my watch. I thought for a moment. "How about this?" I put my fingers in my mouth and whistled loudly.

"Like you said," the Major said, putting his hand on my shoulder, "we're ready."

We ate dinner, which consisted mostly of junk food. I had been in a hurry when I was at the store, and I didn't know what else to get.

"What do you call this?" asked the Private.

"Chocolate-coated beef jerky."

After we had eaten, the old-timers opened their suitcases and cardboard boxes and took out their old, moth-eaten commando uniforms, which were made of camouflage material. I guess there are some things you just never throw away.

"Put this on," said the Major, throwing me a camouflage shirt and a camouflage cloth cap. I put them on. I fastened my Spitzer medal on my shirt pocket, the same place the others wore theirs.

"Walter," said the Major when we had finished dressing. "Your plan for tomorrow is excellent, except for one thing."

"What's that?"

"We need a leader," said the Major. "Someone to lead us into battle."

"What are you talking about? You're the leader of the Spitzers."

"That was long ago, when I was much younger." The Major reached into his pocket and took out something. "We had a talk when you were at the store. We want *you*, Walter, to be our leader." The Major opened his hand, exposing four small brass stars. "You are officially promoted to the rank of General."

"Me? You must be kidding?"

"This is no joke, Walter."

"Wait a minute," I said, stepping back. "Sure, I can come up with a plan, a strategy, but being a leader is something else. I'll just mess things up. You know me. I'm Butterfingers, remember?"

"Not anymore." The Major stepped forward and pinned the four stars on the front of my cap.

"Are you guys sure?" I asked. "Are you sure you want *me* to be the leader of the Spitzers?"

The three men in uniform saluted me, and they held their salutes until I saluted back.

11
The Battle

As the sun began to rise, all was quiet on Felton Street, except for the sound of the early morning wind as it swirled the leaves into giant circles on the lawn out front of the old, run-down house.

Inside the house, the four of us waited in silence, passing Coke and doughnuts back and forth for breakfast.

"What if they don't come?" said the Private in a whisper.

"They'll come," I said.

"We're ready for them!" said the Corporal.

"Quiet," said the Major. "I think I hear something."

We all listened, but it was nothing.

We continued to wait.

I was the first to hear it — the low moan of a large truck off in the distance. It sounded like some wounded animal who had picked up our scent and was heading our way.

"Take your posts."

The men moved at once. There was no hesitation. I had given them an order.

"Remember," I called after them. "First whistle is for the Major. Second whistle, Corporal Kimball. Third, Private Patterson. And when you hear the bugle?"

"Charge!" said the men.

I went with Private Patterson, helping him out the back door and down the steps. I quickly assembled the tank around him. I stuffed a towel into the bucket and put it on his head. I fixed a small American flag on top with tape. Private Patterson was ready.

Back in the house, the Major was manning the hose in the living room. "How's it look?" I asked him.

"Leaking a little," said the Major, "but it'll hold." Major Maddock was ready.

Up on the roof, I found the Corporal leaning up against the railing. He didn't look very good. "You okay?"

"Those stairs are killers."

"How's your throwing arm?"

"Never felt better." The Corporal moved his arm through the air. Corporal Kimball was ready.

I hurried back down the stairs (being careful to use the banister), and out the back door, letting the screen bang.

As I made my way across the open area between the house and the garage, I caught my first glimpse of the enemy. Awesome was the only word for it. Mounted on the back of a truck, the wrecking ball stood three stories high.

"We've got to stop that?" I gulped. The Corporal was right; we needed an air strike.

Inside the garage, I looked through a crack in the garage door just as the wrecking ball pulled up in front of the house. The fat man was driving, the ever present cigar butt clenched in his teeth.

I should have been ready by now, but I wasn't. I had to hurry. I quickly tied the Spitzer bugle to my belt. I unscrewed the cap to the gasoline can, which I had filled earlier with water, stuffed in a piece of cloth, leaving a small tail hanging out, and put the can into an old pillowcase. I felt my right pocket to make sure the cigarette lighter was there. It was. I was ready.

Looking through the crack again, I saw the wrecking ball moving across the front lawn toward the house, its steel-frame tower creaking noisily.

"Come on," I whispered. "A little closer." The fat man brought the truck to a stop directly in front of the living room window. "Perfect," I squealed, putting my hand over my mouth to muffle the sound.

Just then Ralph Britt pulled his long, black Cadillac into the driveway and drove up to within inches of the garage. He got out, looking like a tap dancer in black pants and a white, fluffy shirt. He was so close to me I could have spit on him.

"What are you waiting for?" he yelled at the fat man. "Smash it down."

The fat man took the cigar butt out of his mouth. "I was waiting for you. You're late."

"I'm here now, aren't I? You have eyes. You can see me."

I could tell the fat man didn't like being talked to like that. He threw his cigar butt on the ground, climbed into the back of the truck, and sat down behind the controls to the wrecking ball. He reached for a lever and pulled it. The heavy iron ball, suspended on a long cable, swung into action.

"Now." I put my fingers in my mouth and whistled, putting my mouth as close to the crack in the garage door as possible.

I know it was loud because when I looked again, I saw Ralph holding his ear. I also saw a stream of water coming from the house, right into the face of the fat man. The Major had scored a direct hit.

My second whistle caused the lawn area around the wrecking ball to explode into blobs of brown and yellow and blue paint. The Corporal soon found his range. The fat man took a direct hit to the chest.

A third whistle brought Private Patterson into action, his tank emerging from behind the house, the tiny American flag on his helmet blowing in the wind.

As he passed the garage, I ran out carrying my heavy pillowcase and got behind him. When we got to the front lawn, I could see that the fat man had gotten down from the wrecking ball and was standing way back near the street, out of range of both the Major's cannon and the Corporal's grenades. Ralph was standing next to him. Both looked mad. I mean *really mad*.

"Get the boy!" I heard Ralph shout as he pointed his finger at me. "He's put them up to this."

The fat man picked up something off the ground and came running right at me and Private Patterson.

"Oh, no!" I cried out when I recognized what it was. "He's got a sledge hammer."

"Leave him to me," came the voice of the Private from underneath his bucket. "That's my job."

"But you'll get hurt," I said.

"Won't be the first time."

The fat man was almost on top of us when the lawn exploded again with paint bombs. I left the Private to meet his fate and ran toward the wrecking ball. If we were going to win, each of us had to do his job, and that included me.

I looked back only when I heard the crash of sledge hammer against metal. I saw the tank on its side, wheels spinning. I saw the fat man heading my way.

I turned back around to find Ralph running at me from the opposite direction, his long arms outstretched, his fingernails ready to scratch and tear me apart.

He would have, too, if it weren't for a blast of water that hit him in the face, followed by a paint bomb that hit him on the head. Two direct hits.

I twisted my body trying to get out of the way, tripped, and fell sideways, which was lucky because it caused Ralph and the fat man to run head on into each other.

Getting to my feet, I quickly climbed up into the back of the truck and sat down behind the controls to the wrecking ball. I still had the pillowcase concealing the gasoline can in my hand and the Spitzer bugle tied to my belt. So far, so good.

12
Victory?

"Get down from there," said Ralph, his hair caked with yellow paint.

"I'll get him down," said the fat man as he started to pull himself up into the truck with his strong arms.

"No, you don't," I said, holding up the gasoline can in one hand and the cigarette lighter in the other. I gave the lighter a flick, and a long flame shot into the air, terribly close to the cloth fuse dangling down. "One more step and I'll blow it up."

The fat man stepped back down. He stood next to Ralph.

It was a stalemate, a tie, not good enough to win. I knew that. To win involved offense, an attack, and that is exactly what they were going to get.

I extinguished the lighter. I untied the bugle from my waist and brought it to my lips. I blew. Nothing happened. I blew again. Still nothing. Instead of trying to figure out what was wrong, I opened my mouth and screamed at the top of my lungs, *"CHARGE."*

The front door of the house burst open and out ran Major Maddock and Corporal Kimball, the Corporal limping badly, choosing not to use his cane. Dressed in their commando outfits, their faces smeared with black shoe polish, they looked menacing — especially when they aimed their black pistols at Ralph and the fat man.

Now it was my turn. I lit the fuse to the "gasoline bomb." "Hey, Ralph," I said. "Catch." I threw it at him.

You should have seen Ralph and the fat man take off running. They climbed over each other as they scrambled into Ralph's long, black Cadillac and shot out of there, going in reverse out of the driveway, then continuing in reverse down Felton Street at about sixty miles per hour.

"Yaaahooo!" I yelled at the top of my lungs.

It was checkmate. We had won.

The wrecking ball was still operating so I pushed a button, trying to shut it off.

"Patterson's okay," I heard the Major yell. "Sleeping like a baby."

"Good," I yelled back over the sounds of the wrecking ball as it continued to swing out of control. I pulled another lever. Pushed another button. There had to be some way to shut this thing off.

"Your 'gas bomb' did it," I heard Corporal Kimball say, and I looked over to see him drinking out of the gasoline can. "Best darn gas I've ever tasted."

That's when we started to laugh. I mean, we laughed so hard we couldn't see straight. In fact, we'd probably still be laughing if it weren't for the crash — the first of many crashes.

The wrecking ball was smashing down the house, and there wasn't a thing I could do to stop it. No matter what button I pushed or what lever I pulled, the wrecking ball just kept on smashing and smashing into that old, run-down house until there was nothing left but a big pile of wood and plaster.

I was so mad, I kicked the first thing I saw, which just happened to be the sacred Spitzer bugle.

The bugle sailed high into the air, and as it did, a white piece of paper came out of the end of it and floated down to the ground, coming to rest at the feet of Major Maddock, Corporal Kimball, and Private Patterson.

The Major stooped over and picked up the piece of paper. "Walter," he said, looking up at me, "it's the missing copy of General Britt's will."

Epilogue

LAST WILL AND TESTAMENT OF GENERAL L. R. BRITT

I leave to my good friends Major Maddock, Corporal Kimball, and Private Patterson all my worldly possessions, which include my bank account, the house on Felton Street, and my brother's mansion on Strawberry Hill.

My brother left me the mansion when he died, but I chose to live in the old house on Felton Street because it had so many fond memories for me. You three, however, may wish to move into the mansion. The choice is yours. My poor nephew, Ralph, whom my brother cut off without a cent, is currently living there with my permission, but he has given me his word to go along with whatever you decide.

I would like to trust Ralph. Trust, in my opinion, is the only hope for the world — without it we're left to the lawyers — but I'm no fool; therefore I've left a back-up copy of this will in a place where you are sure to find it.

Good-by, dear friends,
L. R. Britt

P.S. That mansion is so darn big; maybe you should think about turning it into a rest home for aging vets and rescue some of those poor souls down at the hospital. It seems like something the Spitzers would do.